THE SCARIEST MOON

THANVANTH. S. S

Contents

PREFACE

This book, The Scariest moon is a depiction of my own interest in the feild of Horror story writing. This is my first try and the experience of creating a book is very useful.This book includes many mysteries and smooth flow of plot. It has interesting characters and inducing puzzles for the readers to know more.

Book Description

This book describes the horror adventure of a widowed family who return to their ancestral property at Houston. There they get to know about the Spookiest mystery about the Scariest moon at Houston.

What was the history?

What does the Scariest moon mean ?

Read this interesting horror story to unravel the dark history of the past..

ℿ

ACKNOWLEDGEMENTS

This book guarentees the reader horror filled seconds in every page. As an author, I never wish to hurt or pin-point any human or wrong doings. The characters and events of the story are completely imaginery.
I would like to thank every supporter of this small action, and look forward to more support from everyone.

Author's Biography

I, Thanvanth SS, am a student who loves to express my thoughts and imagination to the society through my paintings and stories. The scariest moon is my first attempt in publishing my stories. I am cery interestedvin art, craft and also other curricular and extra curricular activities. I look forward to more appreciation from the world outside.

I

Return from London

During the 1900s , in the famous place of London there lived a small family of 4 members - **John, Iris and their children Kate and Sofia.**

It was 1920, when the Influenza pandemic broke out around the world killing thousands of people and lakhs sick. Poor John also got affected by this severe illness and died by time. Losing her husband, Iris and her children decided to settle along their ancestral property which was in Houston, USA.

As iris was in a job, that she couldn't leave off in the middle, they stayed in London for a year and left to Houston on September 1921. John's ancestors were a long line of kings who ruled that place. Their house in was a big grand palace and a large garden surrounding it.

II

The Spooky Palace

The place was not cleaned for lots and lots of decades, it looked so spooky and scary. Kate and Sofia were really got afraid to see their home. This is the first time they are visiting this place. They found a grandma who was cleaning the lawn.

Sofia went near her and spoke to her so softly. Grandma's eyes lit up with joy when she saw Kate and Sofia... She rushes to Iris and asks whether are they from they from the Dialen dynasty? . Iris nods her head and enquired whether she knew her husband.

Grandma made them sit by the bench and told her about John's ancestors. Iris also asked her how she was related to them? And why was she here...

Grandma said, "My ancestors were servants below the Dialen kings... We were maintaining this palace after Sir Duston Dialen left this palace after being defeated by King Fredrick Adam in the 1728."

As we don't have the key to, the palace and as she was too old, she could not maintain the Palace, but the garden was very well maintained by her. Iris told her that they, from now on were going to live In Houston and that she has to find a job. The old lady said that they can manage everything. Iris had the key, which John kept insisting her to keep safe. And now opened the gates of the Palace, by the little hands of Sofia and Kate

III

Life in Houston

By a month they were done with all the cleaning and setting and even iris found a new job. The kids were also going to school by then. Their life in Houston started peacefully.

The Palace Room

On a full moon day, while Iris was back from work and was on her way back from school after picking up her kids, they noticed that the full moon was not as a usual moon they see in London, it appeared as if a ghost has taken over moon. It was so terrifying that they soon got home and never looked at the moon that day. Next morning it was a holiday for the kids. They went to the nearby park for Playing, by the time Iris went to the Old lady and asked about the moon's unusual phenomena.

The old lady just replied her that she will give her a secret when time comes and asked her not to ask about the moon again. As time passed Iris noted that the moon was very terrifying on every full moon day.

IV

The Disaster

It was February 10, 1922. The old lady came up to Iris and told her that not to go out anywhere tomorrow. And to just stay back at home. When iris asked her the reason, she said that tomorrow there will be a huge disaster attacking over Houston and destroying everything around it.

Iris could not understand anything, but obeyed her words. Next day dawned and as the old lady said enormous dark clouds covered Houston and there was not even a crow to be seen on the streets. Iris sensed some disaster approaching she quickly came out and bought the Old lady inside the palace. And then it started Storming. Thunderstorms plucked out the trees and threw them far way. The streets were flooded with water and low-lying areas were suffering a lot. Iris offered the Lady a hot Coffee and asked her how did she predict this yesterday itself?

The old lady said that it was the time to tell her the secret about the spooky moon and a long History behind it. Grandma said,

"*To Find The Truth , Read the Chapter*
THE PAST ...."

V

THE PAST - The War of 1727

"Long ago, there lived a wealthy and rich King from the dynasty of Adam, his name was Fredrick Adam and he ruled over Houston which was a big country by then.

He had an enemy, from the Dynasty of Dialens (John's dynasty) and the King's name was Duston Dialen.

By the year of 1727, A war arose between Adams and Dialens, the war was very ferocious and full-fledged. As the Adams had more Power they won, and the Dialen king's kingdom was taken over, therefore Duston Dialen went to London and began their Livelihood there as businessmen. This was how John was away from Houston.

Enter Caption

Within a year of their victory in 1729 Fredrick Adam died and his only son Fruis Adam took over the throne. He had a wife, Melina Fruis and a son and Daughter - Nicholas Adam and Merilia Adam.

Fruis Adam & Family

VI

THE PAST - The Mystery Girl

'Merilia used to play by a nearby park, in which, along a bench sat a gloomy girl in White frock. Everyday, she will arrive before Merilia comes and leaves after Merilia leaves. No one knows who she is and where she is from. She will neither speak to anyone nor play.

"After much questions from Merilia daily, finally she was only able to get her name, which was AURORA'."

Nicholas got eager to know about her, so he stayed back at the park secretly, when it was 7.00 PM and moon was beginning to shine bright, Aurora stood up and left the park, Nicholas was secretly following her, It led him to a mountain top from where Aurora grew wings and flew away and vanished into the moon. Nicholas could not believe his eyes. Next morning, he came again to the top where she vanished from, when it was the time for the moon to set and sun to rise Aurora came back from the moon to the mountain top and her wings disappeared. She walked back to the park and sat at her usual place. Nicholas was super shocked.

VII

THE PAST - The Book

Fedrick Adam's Room

Nicholas went back to his home and told this incident to Merilia. Fruis also got to know about this,Fruis rushed towards his father's room and opened an old locker, which his father said was a collection of true stories about Fairies and Magics collected and preserved from the times of their Ruling era.

Fruis found a book, named 'The Moon Fairies' When he read it, he came to know that Aurora was the daughter of the Moon Queen Blairaide. Aurora was the 93rd heir of the moon's Throne.

He also read that if a person has to live for 100 years and his dynasty should never be destroyed from their King's rule, the present king has to make a Ritual for the God of death with the blood drips of Moon Queen and princess.

VIII
THE PAST - The Curse

After reading these, Fruis got more jealous and greedier to deserve them. And as it is written, Fruis ordered the guards to capture Aurora and bring her to him, then he took her to the hill top which Nicholas said, she used to vanish from and shouted looking at the moon, "Oh Queen of the Moon! I have your daughter as my Hostage and if you don't come down, I will kill her.". The queen sitting on the moon, heard these words and rushed to the earth...

As soon as she came to the hill top, Fruis stabbed her from the back and Aurora too. As it was night and moon light fell on the corpses of the queen and princess, their spirit rose from their bodies and spoke to Fruis, "Oh Evil King! Today you have killed us and we won't leave you as it is. On every full moon day in Houston, Aurora would appear as a terrifying face of moon and keep telling you the worst thing you have ever done in your life.

Moon Queen to the Earth

And me, being the queen, would reappear after every 6 years on the same date and day as a huge thunderstorm and destroy your whole kingdom, which will affect the lives of people of your kingdom. And I pledge that I would not spare even a single life of your Dynasty."

This made Fruis more terrified, but he wanted to continue with the ritual. But even the ritual was not performed good. The spirits of Aurora and Blairaide, threw away the things and they couldn't even lit up the fire. And as the time was passing the blood of the queen and princess turned black and their corpses decomposed into the air.

As per the book's saying once the bloods turn black, the ritual is useless. Fruis got a curse and nothing was a gain. Fruis was heartbroken, and as the curse said, every full moon in Houston the moon looked terrifying, spreading negative vibes over his country. And after 6 years, when feb 11 fell on a Saturday again, huge thunderstorms and cyclones gathered over Houston, uprooting trees and it was the most Disastrous day Houston ever saw.

During that day, none of the poor people or others died, but just got harm. But Fruis's palace was totally damaged and everyone in the family died within the same day. As the spirit was not calm even by then, It continued to destroy the livelihoods of people in Houston every six years after that."

And here ended the sad history of Moon queen Blairaide and Aurora.

IX

Who is the Girl ?

Iris was really shocked to hear such a story. She asked whether the curse could be solved by performing any ritual or not. Grandma said that there was only one way to solve this issue and rescue Houston from these ferocious spirits. It was that, there was a belief that Aurora would reappear as a normal Human being and come to Houston one day

We must find her and perform a ritual to the moon on a full moon day, if the moon gets happy, the terrifying cover gets vanished and the spirits will never interfere with Houston anymore.

When Iris asked that, why being so many years did the people never did this ? Grandma said that they tried so hard but Aurora was not be found anywhere. Iris also asked that whether there was any symbolic identity for Aurora ? Grandma replied with a strong "YES" continuing that we

could find a half moon, which will appear on her neck during the time of Disaster by recognizing her mother.

Iris came to know that it was impossible even to go out during that storm, and how could they find the girl on time.

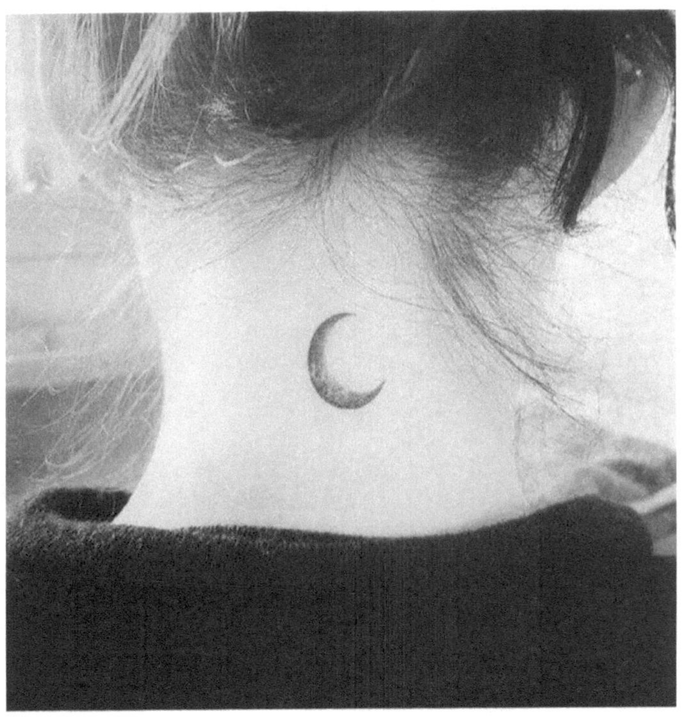

Half Moon on Sofia's Neck

By the time, Sofia came crying to her mother, she said that something was paining in her neck, when iris swept her hair and took a look, Both Iris and Grandma were super-duper Shocked!

Aurora 's Rebirth is Sofia

They found the shining moon on Sofia's neck!
She was Aurora's rebirth.

• 26 •

X
The Ritual

Moon Light from Window

Without wasting anytime, they prepared for a small ritual near the window of the living room, from where the moon's light was entering into the room.

And as the grandma read the mantra of moon, Iris lit up a fire, and as soon as the fire began to flame up, the thunder slowed down and became calm.

And by the end, there rose a black spirit from the flames, it was Blairaide, she did nothing but kissed Sofia, a white spirit rose from Sofia, it was Aurora, they both thanked Iris and Grandma and flied back to the moon.

Blairaide Rose from the fire

Happy Houston

The next day in Houston was a very happy day. Iris has informed about the spirits and confirmed that the spirits, would never ever torture Houston anymore. Every people were so happy to hear this.

They rejoiced this celebration and in memory of this auspicious day, on every full moon day, the people of Houston offered prayers to moon for calming down.

The next full moon which appeared on Houston was as beautiful as it could ever be. White like Milk and soft like Silk. A boon to the viewer's eyes. The Scariest moon turnd into a gorgeous moon.

The End.............

9 7 9 8 8 8 6 8 4 3 2 8 6